Disney · PIXAR

WALL·E

Illustrated by Art Mawhinney and the Disney Storybook Artists

Published by Louis Weber, C.E.O.
Publications International, Ltd.
7373 North Cicero Avenue, Lincolnwood, Illinois 60712
Ground Floor, 59 Gloucester Place, London W1U 8JJ

Customer Service: 1-800-595-8484
or customer_service@pilbooks.com

www.pilbooks.com

Manufactured in China.

p i kids is a registered trademark of Publications International, Ltd.
Look and Find is a registered trademark of Publications International, Ltd.,
in the United States and in Canada.

8 7 6 5 4 3 2 1

ISBN-13: 978-1-4127-7456-7
ISBN-10: 1-4127-7456-X

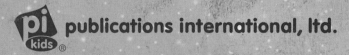

publications international, ltd.

WALL•E's job is to clean up Earth. As he makes cubes of garbage and stacks them high, look for these pieces of trash.

Newspaper

Rubber duck

Refrigerator

Bottle

Fire extinguisher

Boot

Shopping cart

A probe-bot named EVE has come to Earth to search for life. Soon she and WALL•E become friends, and WALL•E takes her home. Look around the truck to find these prized possessions WALL•E is proud to show EVE.

Pinwheel

Hand mixer

Clock

Ring box

Lightbulb

Tree lights

Videotape

When EVE's ship came to take her – and the plant – away from Earth, WALL•E hitched a ride. Now they're aboard a starliner called the *Axiom*. As WALL•E tries to follow EVE, look for these robots that are getting in the way.

GO-4

Beautician-bot

Vacuum-bot

Massage-bot

M-O

Paint-bot

Umbrella-bot

WALL•E continues to chase EVE through the passenger level of the *Axiom*. He has never seen anything like this! Can you find these different shops and services?

FOOD
CONSUMPTION JUNCTION

BnL
FLUSHABLES

MILIPLEX
1000

CUP OF FOODS
BnL

ALL NITE
CAFÉ

DISPOSE 'N' GO

International House of
CONDIMENTS

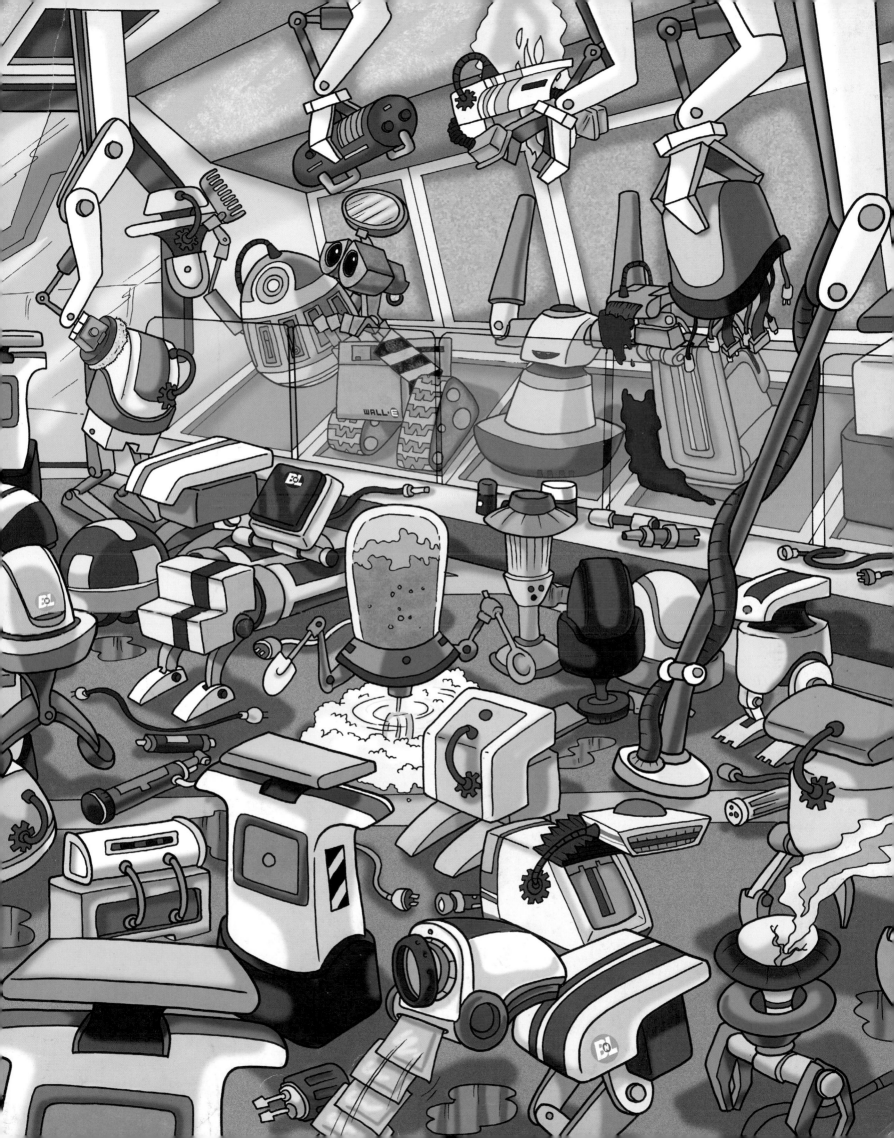

WALL•E and EVE have fallen down the garbage chute and into a sea of trash. Look around the massive piles of garbage for these old items the trash-compacting WALL•As are about to cube up and send into space.

Bottle

Tin can

Winter coat

Futuristic news device

Rocking horse

Food cup

BnL shirt

The ship's passengers are being prepared for the *Axiom's* return to Earth, but everything's gone a little haywire. See if you can spot these passengers in the hubbub.

John

Mary

Ron

Geri

Larry

Carrie

Lon

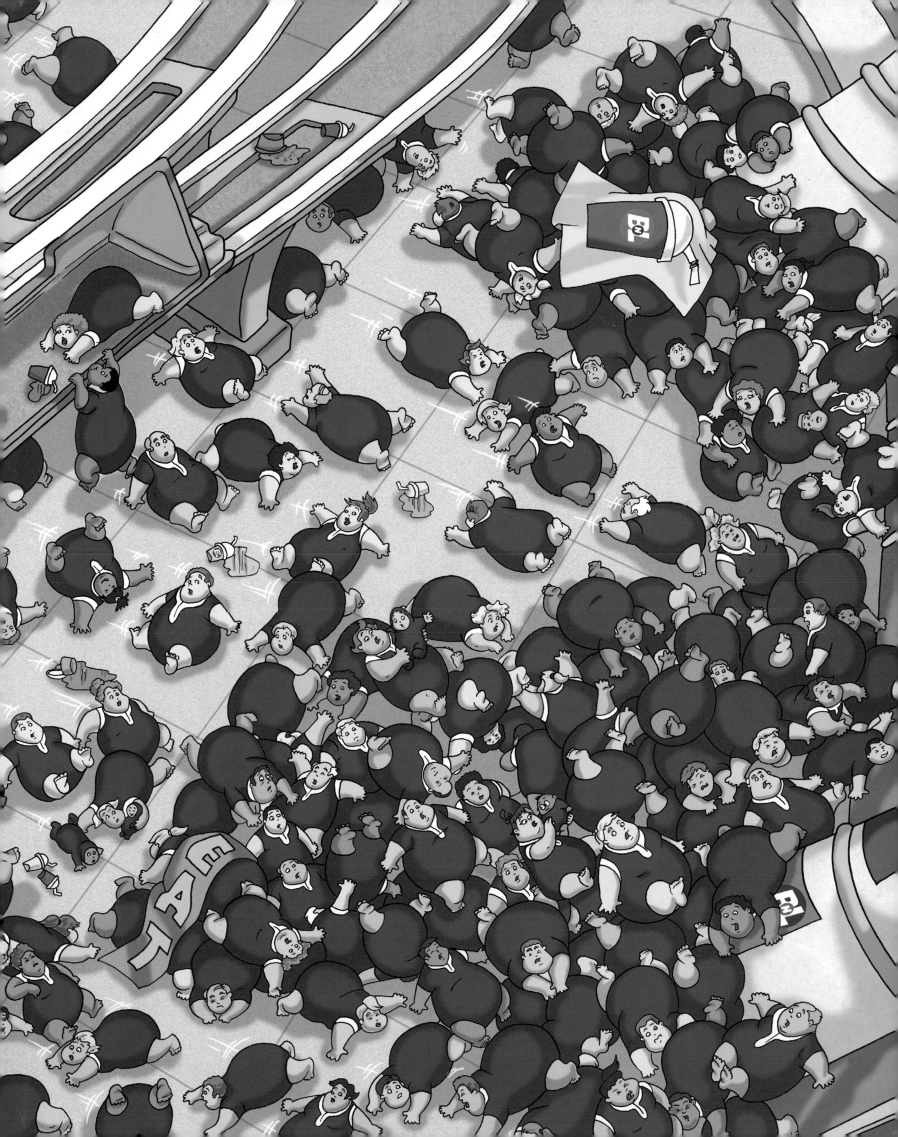

The *Axiom* has returned to Earth at last! It isn't perfect here yet, but the Captain and his passengers are hopeful. In fact, there seems to be more life already. Look for these plants that sprang up while WALL•E was away.

Daisy

Bean sprout

Dandelion

Rosebush

Vine

Fern

Poppy

WALL•E loves to collect the most interesting bits of junk. But he has his own idea of what's valuable. Go back to the work site and find these things that WALL•E didn't think were worth keeping.

Gold coin

Diamond ring

Money

Vase

Jeweled necklace

Gold watch

WALL•E loves music, especially music about love! Visit WALL•E's home again to find these musical things.

Boom box

CD

Sheet music

Record

Harmonica

Cassette tape

Zoom back to the *Axiom's* busy corridors and see if you can spot these robots.

Defibrillator-bot

This steward-bot

Valet-bot

Camera-bot

Fan-bot

Cook-bot

Mmmm! Lunch in a cup! Glide back to the *Axiom* to find the passengers' favorite eateries.

BUCKET O' CHICKEN
CARBS!
CAR-BO-LAND GROCERY
FREEZE DRIED FAVORITES
CHICKEN OF THE SPACE
SLURP 'N GO
TACO CUP

Motor your way back to the Repair Ward and look for these tools used to clean and fix up defective robots.

Buffer

Touch-up spray paint

Alpha beta stabilizer

Squeegee

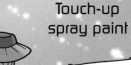
Holographic scan detector

Circuit analyzer

Diagnostic emitter

Leap back down the garbage chute and search for more items that the *Axiom's* passengers no longer needed.

Boots

Fork

Virtual book

Mittens

Sunglasses

Toothbrush

File back to the people pile and look for six Buy n Large logos among the toppled passengers.

BNL

The return of plants on Earth offers hope for the future, but there's still a lot to be done. Look around the *Axiom's* homecoming for this junk that WALL•E will need to clear.

Axiom brochure

Soft drink

Shopping bag

T-shirt

Sign

Pizza box